JPict
D   , A

Translated from the French by Claudia Zoe Bedrick

enchantedlion.com

First published in 2017 by Enchanted Lion Books,
67 West Street, 317A, Brooklyn, NY 11222

Originally published in French as *La Chose*
Copyright © 2015, Editions Nathan, SEJER, Paris – France
Copyright © 2017 by Enchanted Lion Books for the English-language translation
Copyediting and layout for English edition: Lawrence Kim

ISBN 978-1-59270-217-6

Printed in France

First Printing

Astrid Desbordes

Marc Boutavant

Edmond
The thing

ENCHANTED LION BOOKS

NEW YORK

One autumn afternoon, Edmond the Squirrel and
his friend George Owl went for a walk along the river.
George, who loved disguises and dressing up,
was collecting moss and leaves for a new costume.

SKRAWK. Suddenly, George and Edmond heard a strange sound.

"What's that?" whispered George, his eyes widening.

On the other side of the river, a Thing with a beak and shiny fur was staring straight at them.

"I don't know," whispered Edmond, drawing back a little.

SKRAWK, went the Thing again, its eyes still fixed on them.

The two friends ran as fast as they could, all the way back to Edmond's house. From behind the shutters, they watched the Thing.

"What should we do?" asked George. "This is clearly a very dangerous Thing."

"We have to be brave," replied Edmond, trembling.

"B-b-brave?" repeated George.

Edmond pulled out a box of green cookies to help calm them down.

When the box of cookies was nearly empty,
George declared, "I'm feeling a little braver now.
Brave enough to go home to bed."

Edmond, though, had other plans.
He went down to the river and posted a big sign.

At home, George Owl consulted *The Big Encyclopedia of the Forest*. He searched for "Thing" but found nothing.

He climbed into bed and pulled up the covers.

In the morning, George felt much braver than he had the day before. "It must have been those green cookies," he said to himself.

Curious, he decided to go see if the Thing was still there. "But I won't go as I am," he told himself. "That would be too dangerous. I'll go disguised as something scary instead."

On his way to the river, George bumped into his neighbors—the mice Polka and Hortense, Louis the Rabbit, and Edward the Bear. As soon as they saw him, they ran away screaming, without giving him a second look or a chance to explain.

Delighted by the effect of his costume, George knocked on Edmond's window.

"Ahhhhhhh!" cried Edmond.

"It's me, George!"

"Ahhhhhhh!" cried Edmond again.

"Come on, stop it!" said George impatiently. "Listen. It's really me."

"*Go away!*" wailed Edmond.

George, shaken, made his way to the river. He sat down
to think.

"It must not be easy being the Thing," he thought.

SKRAWK, went the Thing, moving its hands.

"Um … hello," replied George. "Hello."

George and the Thing looked at each other for a long time.

"I'm sorry, George," said Edmond, joining his friend. "I didn't recognize you under all that moss."

"Oh, it doesn't matter," said George. "I understand. But it's funny—the Thing isn't afraid of me at all."

Turning around, Edmond saw the Thing.

"Oh … um … Thing!" Edmond's voice trembled. "Um … would you like a green cookie?"

They shared some cookies, and as they ate,
Edmond thought. Then he thought a little more.

Carefully, he took down the sign and laid it across
the river to make a bridge.

After a few more cookies, George, who had also been thinking, confessed, "You know, I don't think green cookies and feeling brave have very much to do with each other at all."

The sun was almost setting by the time the three friends said goodbye.

SKRAWK, said the Thing as he went on his way.

"See you soon!" George and Edmond called after him.

When George got home, he opened his encyclopedia.

On the page beginning with "squirrel," he carefully added "Thing" at the bottom.

"This encyclopedia is truly complete," he said, closing the book. "At least for now."

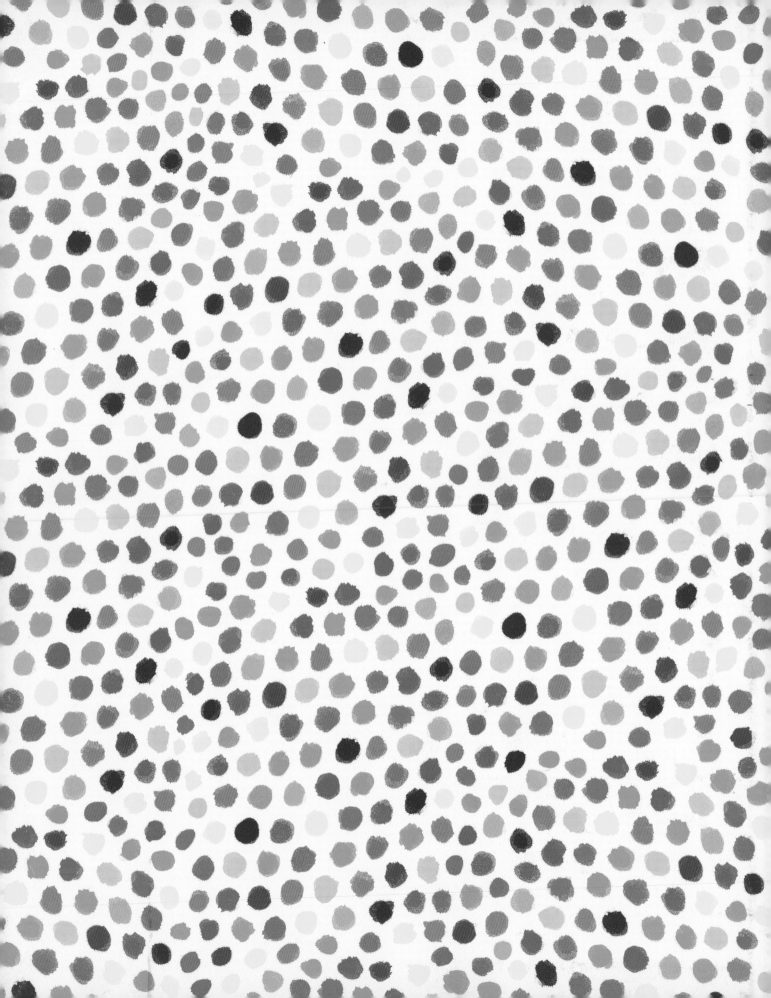